Harriet Lerner and Susan Goldhor

Franny B. Kranny, There's a Bird in Your Hair!

Illustrated by Helen Oxenbury

HarperCollinsPublishers

To my Worley-Bird, aka Jo-Lynne Worley

—H.L.

To my husband, Aron Bernstein

—S.G.

and to Phyllis Rubin, the *real* Aunt Phyllis

—S.G. and H.L.

Franny B. Kranny, There's a Bird in Your Hair!

Text copyright © 2001 by Harriet Lerner and Susan Goldhor

Illustrations copyright © 2001 by Helen Oxenbury

All rights reserved. Printed in Singapore.

www.harperchildrens.com

Library of Congress Cataloging-in-Publication Data

Lerner, Harriet Goldhor.

Franny B. Kranny, there's a bird in your hair! / by Harriet Lerner and Susan Goldhor;

illustrated by Helen Oxenbury.

p.   cm.

Summary: Franny B. Kranny refuses to cut her wild hair, despite her family's insistence,

and wears a bird in her hair to a family reunion.

ISBN 0-06-024683-9 – ISBN 0-06-029503-1 (lib. bdg.) – ISBN 0-06-051785-9 (pbk.)

[1. Hair–Fiction. 2. Birds–Fiction. 3. Family reunions–Fiction.] I. Goldhor, Susan.

II. Oxenbury, Helen, ill. III. Title.

PZ7.L5595Fr   2000   97-42821

[E]–dc21

Typography by Al Cetta

❖

Franny B. Kranny had long, frizzy hair.
It was always getting her in trouble.
Franny B. Kranny's hair tied itself in
knots on the buttons of her dress.

Franny B. Kranny's hair made the girl
sitting next to her on the school bus
sneeze every day on the way to school.

Franny B. Kranny's hair even got stuck in the refrigerator door.

But Franny B. Kranny loved her long, frizzy hair. The longer and frizzier it got, the more she liked it.

Franny B. Kranny thought her long, frizzy hair was beautiful. She could brush it down in front of her face and pretend she was in a cave.

She loved to press her hair flat
against her head and watch it
boing out again.

Franny B. Kranny's mother was very tired of untangling all this long, frizzy hair.

"Wouldn't you like nice, neat, short, pretty hair like your sister Bertha's?" she asked.

"No!" said Franny B. Kranny.

"I think you would look so pretty with short hair," said Franny B. Kranny's father.

"I think so too!" said Bertha.

"No!" said Franny B. Kranny.

One day Franny B. Kranny's parents announced that there was going to be a big family reunion. All their relatives would be coming.

"And," said Franny B. Kranny's mother, "the day before the party you are both going to the hairdresser."

"I'm going to get my hair curled," said Bertha proudly.

"Not me," said Franny B. Kranny. "I don't want anyone touching my hair."

"We'll see," said Franny B. Kranny's mother.

Before Franny B. Kranny knew it, the day before the party had come. Her mother told the hairdresser exactly what she wanted him to do with Franny B. Kranny's hair.

"Pin it up on her head and make it neat," she said.

"You have very interesting hair, young lady," the hairdresser said politely. He had never seen anything like it before.

Franny B. Kranny didn't like him one bit. She closed her eyes, shut her mouth, and crossed her arms. She did not say one word to him the whole time he was working on her hair.

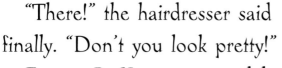

"There!" the hairdresser said finally. "Don't you look pretty!"

Franny B. Kranny opened her eyes. Her long, frizzy hair was piled on top of her head in a giant heap.

"Very nice," said her mother.

"At least it won't fly around and get caught in the cake," said Bertha.

Franny B. Kranny didn't say anything. She just stared into the mirror, thinking about the best way to undo her new hairdo.

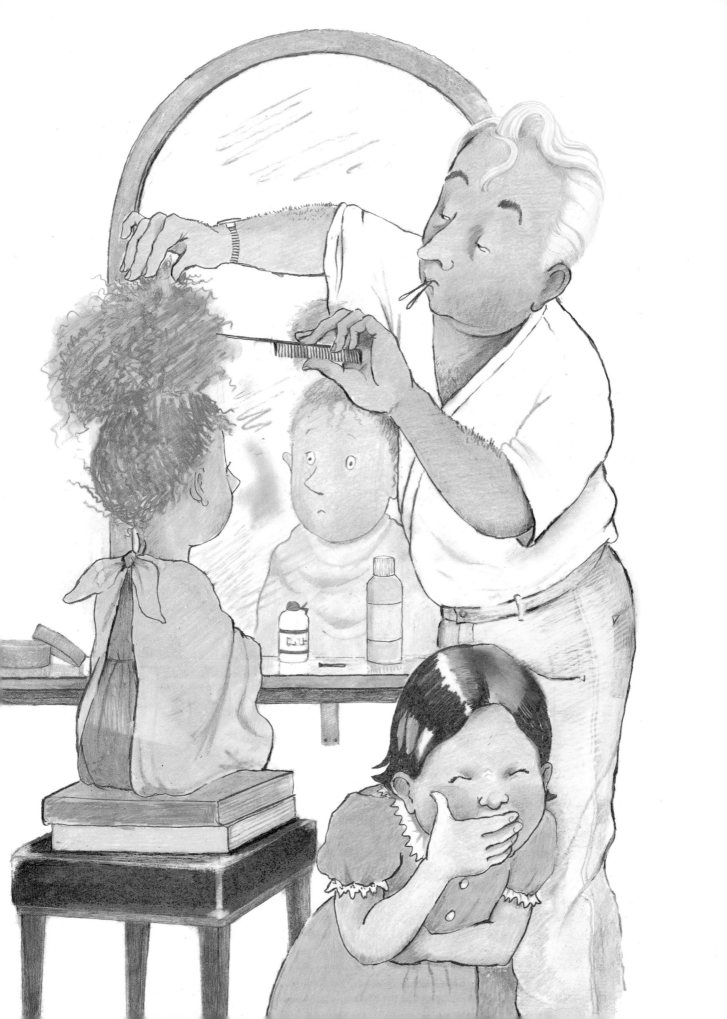

Franny B. Kranny was walking slowly home behind her mother and Bertha, thinking and thinking, when suddenly something amazing happened. A brown bird flew down from a nearby tree and landed in the middle of Franny B. Kranny's new hairdo.

Her mother screamed, and Bertha jumped up and down, but the bird would not budge. It just snuggled deeper into the pile of long, frizzy hair on the top of Franny B. Kranny's head.

"Don't scare it away," said Franny B. Kranny. "I want it there."

When they reached their front door, the brown bird
was still there.

"Maybe it thinks you're a tree," said Franny B. Kranny's
mother.

"Maybe it thinks your hair is a nest," said Bertha.

"There's a bird in your hair," said Franny B. Kranny's father. "Maybe you should take apart that new hairdo!"

Suddenly Franny B. Kranny was beginning to like her new hairdo.

"No!" said Franny B. Kranny.

At bedtime Franny B. Kranny had to solve some problems. How could she bend over and take off her shoes? Then she remembered the deep knee bends she had learned in gym class.

How was she going to sleep? Then she remembered her father's big armchair.

After everyone was asleep, she tiptoed down the hall and curled up in the chair.

In the morning there were even more problems.

"Time to take a shower!" said Franny B. Kranny's mother.

A shower! thought Franny B. Kranny. *Oh, no!* She decided to take a bath instead and was very careful not to splash water on her head.

Soon it was time for the family reunion.
Bertha was very embarrassed to have a sister
with a bird on her head.

"I'm going to tell everyone I never saw
Franny B. Kranny before in my life!" she
told her parents.

"You look like a birdbrain!" she told
Franny B. Kranny.

But Franny B. Kranny thought she looked beautiful, and she marched proudly into the party with the brown bird perched on the very top of her head.

No one at the family reunion had ever seen a
hairdo like this one! Everyone crowded around
Franny B. Kranny.

Her cousin Ethan, who never smiled, laughed out loud when Franny B. Kranny let him feed the bird a peanut.

Uncle Isadore, who was usually very grouchy, told Franny B. Kranny he was sorry he was bald and couldn't take his favorite pigeon home from the park. It would slide off his head!

Aunt Phyllis, who worked at a television station, thought Franny B. Kranny's hair was NEWS. She called her office and told them to send the cameras.

Bertha was careful to stay very close to Franny B. Kranny so everyone would know they were sisters.

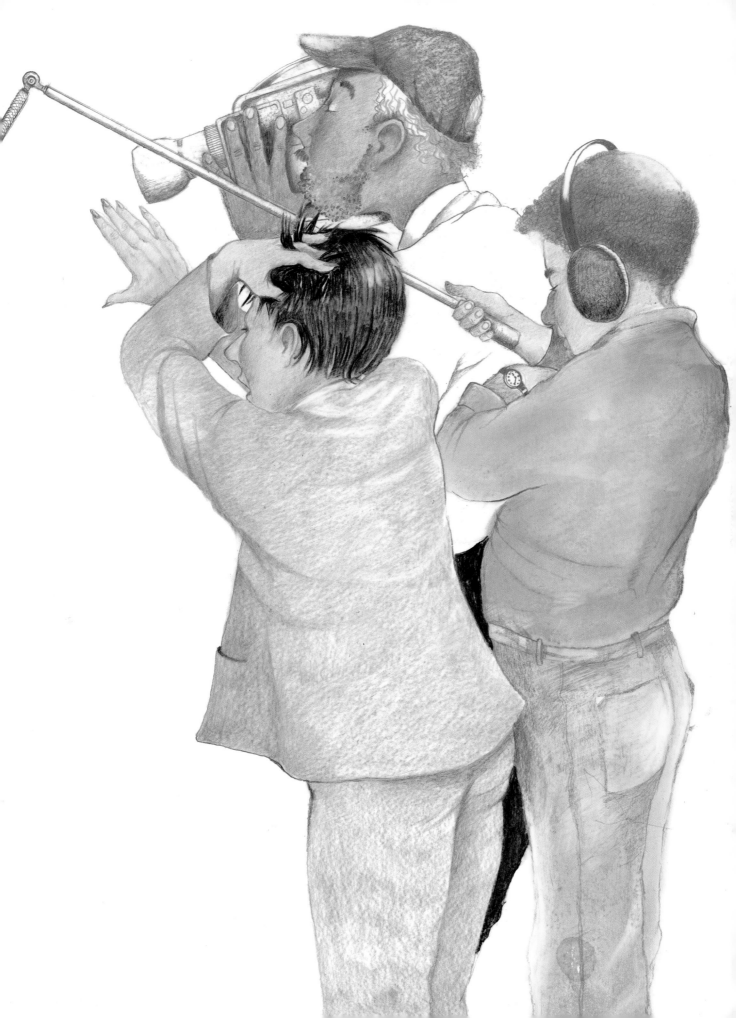

The day after the party Bertha said, "I'm so glad you didn't cut your hair. It's awesome!"

"That's what you think," said Franny B. Kranny. "I'm getting it cut tomorrow!"

"Oh, no!" cried her mother. "You can't do that!"

"Oh, yes," said Franny B. Kranny, "I can."

"Why now?" asked her father.

"A little birdie told me to," said Franny B. Kranny.

HARRIET LERNER is one of the most respected voices on family relationships. Her books include the *New York Times* best-seller THE DANCE OF ANGER and THE MOTHER DANCE: *How Children Change Your Life*. She is a staff psychologist at the Menninger Clinic in Topeka, Kansas. She and her husband have two sons, Matt and Ben. Harriet previously teamed up with big sister Susan Goldhor to co-write the children's book WHAT'S SO TERRIBLE ABOUT SWALLOWING AN APPLE SEED?

SUSAN GOLDHOR is a biologist who has traced mouse movements around a small island, collected sheep-guarding dogs from mountain villages in Turkey, and recycled organic wastes into a variety of products. She lives in Cambridge, Massachusetts, and Tamworth, New Hampshire, with her husband, who is a physicist.

HELEN OXENBURY is one of the world's most popular and acclaimed children's book illustrators. She has won England's Kate Greenaway Medal as well as many other awards. Her recent books include IT'S MY BIRTHDAY, SO MUCH, and ALICE'S ADVENTURES IN WONDERLAND.